With thanks

To Wendy, for whom I started writing stories.

To Ann, whose class made a play out of my story .
When I heard the tape she had made for me
it brought tears to my eyes.

And for Ettie, without whom I would never
have seen my name in print!

The White Elephant

and other stories

The White Elephant

A baby elephant was born one steamy jungle night

The herd turned up their trunks at him and laughed – for he was white.

And when he heard them laugh at him it made him feel ashamed,

Their hides were wrinkled, tough and gray. He longed to look the same.

He asked his Mummy if she knew the way to make him gray;

His mummy said she didn't...but she loved him, anyway!

So, sadly he decided that he'd have to leave the herd,

And find someone to help him, some wise animal or bird .

He wandered through the jungle, far he wandered, day and night

And everyone he saw, he asked, "Please tell me why I'm white?"

He asked a great wise owl he saw, who'd flown there from afar

The owl just blinked and hooted "Be content with what you

are!"

He asked a sssssslimy yellow sssssnake if he could turn him

gray

The ssslimy ssnake just hisssed at him, and ssslowly sslid away

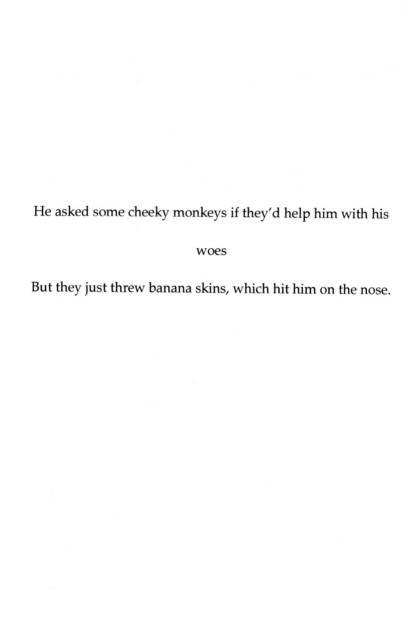

He asked some cheeky monkeys if they'd help him with his

woes

But they just threw banana skins, which hit him on the nose.

He asked a grinning crocodile if he would give advice

The croc just tried to bite his trunk – which wasn't very nice!

He heard some pretty parrots squawking loudly in a tree
He called to them "Stop singing, please, and take a look at me."

The parrots stopped their squawking, but they said "Oh, go away!
What's new about an elephant that's small and fat and gray?"
"I'm gray?" He asked, bewildered, "But I thought that I was white?"
"White elephants? There's no such thing! Now, that WOULD be a sight!"

They laughed and laughed and laughed at him, but he no
longer cared
He hurried to the river, and he stood and stared and stared.
He gazed at his reflection and he could not look away,
For there he was, still small and fat, but now a lovely gray!
He'd walked for miles and miles and miles, until his feet were
sore
Now mud and dust had covered him, and he was white no
more!

And so the little traveler went back the way he'd come

He greeted all the elephants, and hugged his happy mum

The herd was glad to see him, so it all turned out alright

And everybody soon forgot that he had once been WHITE!

The Crocodile's Tears

Once, on the banks of the river Nile, There lived an
unhappy crocodile,
Nobody EVER had seen him smile.
The crocodile just SNAPPED!

When all the children came out to play,
He never had a good word to say,
Never said even, "Hello, nice day!"
The crocodile just SNAPPED

One day the crocodile swam so near

All of the children were filled with fear

Yasmin looked closer, and saw – a tear!

The crocodile just CRIED!

Yasmin was kind and she called, "Poor dear,

Why are you crying?" The croc swam near,

Whispered his sad story in her ear.

The crocodile just CRIED

Yasmin jumped up and she said "That's bad!

I'm going home and I'll get my Dad,

I know he'll help you, so don't be sad."

The crocodile still CRIED

Soon she returned, and she brought her Dad

He was a dentist, and very glad

To pull out croc's tooth, (which was going bad).

The crocodile just SMILED

"I never meant to be bad" said he.

"But I was in so much pain, you see!

That rotten tooth was just killing me!"

The crocodile just SMILED

Now on the banks of the river Nile

Yasmin's best friend is the crocodile.

He plays all day with a great big smile.

The crocodile just SMILES

HANDSOME AND HOMELY

One fine day in early spring
Two birds cleaned their feathered wings
Perched awhile upon a gate
Then flew off to find a mate.
One was Handsome, glossy, neat;
One was Homely, ruffled, sweet.
Through the countryside and towns,
Streets and houses, hills and downs
They searched hopefully, and then
Both birds found the same sweet hen:
Small and fluffy, clean and neat
Sparkling eyes and dainty feet.

Handsome said, "Come live with me!

What a lucky hen you'll be!"

Homely said, his small head bowed,

"Be my mate; I'd be so proud!"

Who should win, and who should lose?

Sparkling eyes just couldn't choose.

So she said, "We'll do a test.

Each of you will build a nest.

He who builds the nicest home,

He will win me for his own."

Homely said, "I'll build mine here
So your friends will all be near."
Handsome said, "I'll fly afar,
Build MY nest among the stars!"
Off he flew on gleaming wings.
Homely stayed, collecting things.
Searching tree and bush and ground
Flying back with all he found.
Tiny feathers from his chest
They would make a cozy nest.
Twigs to make the outside strong,
Flexible, and not too long.
Next he had to choose the tree,
Where the new home was to be.
Sparkling Eyes was always near;
Homely sang, for her to hear.
All day Homely did his best
To build his mate the ideal nest.
Then they heard a boasting voice:
"Now's the time to make your choice"
Gleaming in the setting sun,
Handsome said, "My work is done!

Come with me and see my nest,

Then you'll know which one is best."

Sad of eye, with heavy heart

Homely watched the two depart.

'Till they disappeared from sight,

In the cloudy, stormy night.

Handsome flew through darkening skies

With no thought for Sparkling Eyes,

Though she flew through drenching rain,

Though she felt increasing pain,

Calling, "Are we getting near?"

Handsome didn't even hear.

He flew on, seemed to forget

Sparkling Eyes was cold and wet.

Then at last, he called, "We're here.

There is your new home, my dear."

Pointing to his nest with pride.

Sparkling Eyes looked – then she cried.

Had he really done his best?

What she saw was not a nest,

Just a pile of twigs and sticks,

Much too hard for baby chicks.

No soft feathers from HIS chest

Lined the fast-collapsing nest.

Sticks and twigs stuck in a tree

So low down, that cats could see!

Nests should always be built high,

And they should be warm and dry!

Tired and sad, she shook her head.

"That is not a home," she said.

"I'm too tired to fly tonight,

But I'll leave when it gets light."

For a while the poor hen wept,

Then she closed her eyes, and slept.

She flew off at break of day,

For it was a long, long way.

When she reached her favorite tree

Homely waited, hopefully.

Humbly said, "I did my best;

Do you like my little nest?"

Sparkling Eyes looked then, and saw

High up, far from feline claws

Sheltered from the sun's hot rays,

And the wet and windy days,

Lined with feathers from his chest,

Homely's lovely little nest.

When she blushed, "I'll be your bride."

Homely's chest puffed up with pride.

With their chicks (they hatched out four)

They lived happy ever more.

Made in the USA
Monee, IL
13 September 2021